Manny and

Authors:

Ali R. and Valerie Bustamante

Illustrator:

Monica Lunot-Kuker

Published by Hard Ball Press, December, 2014.
Information available at: www.hardballpress.com
ISBN: 978-0-9911639-4-6
Story by Ali R. & Valerie Bustamante
Illustrations by Monica Lunot-Kuker
Book design by T. Sheard & D. Bass.
Print format by D. Bass

This little book is lovingly dedicated to our son and inspiration, Liam Ali.
—Ali R. and Valerie Bustamante

Manny
and the
Mango Tree

WHO'S
TREE?
'OUR TREE!

Manny woke up early Saturday morning and ran to the window. Were the mangoes finally ready? Could today be the day?

The sweet smell of
mangoes
filled the air.

Manny dashed to tell his mother.

"Mama, Mama, the mangoes are ready!" shouted Manny
with excitement. "They're finally ripe. I can't wait to eat a
sweet juicy mango!"

"Your Papa and I love mangoes too," said Mama. "Let's call
Papa and tell him the good news."

5

After talking on the phone with papa, who was away, Manny thought of all the delicious ways he could eat a mango.

"Mama," he said. "Can I please go to the courtyard and pick a mango?"

"Of course, Manny," said Mama. "Take Maria with you. You both worked very hard for those mangoes."

Manny ran out of the front door and down the stairs, past Mrs. Garcia's dog. He grabbed Maria from her apartment and went outside to the mango tree.

In the courtyard, the children saw a sign nailed to the mango tree.

They read the sign, looked at each other, and could not believe their eyes.

"Manny, Maria, where are your mangoes?" asked Mama when the children returned to the apartment.

With a sigh, the children explained about the sign the Super had put up.

"I fed the mango tree and kept the bugs off the fruit," said Maria."

And I watered the mango tree when it was hot and there was no rain," said Manny.

"Now we can't eat a sweet juicy mango," said Manny. "It's not fair!"

"Oh, children," said Mama as she kissed them on the forehead. "You took very good care of the mango tree all year long. But you have to follow the rules even if you think they're not fair."

In a whisper, Mama added, "Some of the people in our building do not have their papers. We don't want to make trouble, the owner could call immigration and send them back home."

"But Mama," said Manny. "It's not right that one person keeps all the mangoes!"

Mama paused to think. Then she said, "Well, if you ask the super Mr. Grimes in a very polite voice if you can have a mango, maybe he will change his mind."

Manny thought Mr. Grimes would never let him have a sweet juicy mango, but he decided to try, anyway.

Manny and María knocked on the Super's door, feeling nervous as they heard Mr. Grimes' footsteps.

The door swung open and Manny and María looked up.

Mr. Grimes poked his head out and growled, "I'll fix the hot water tomorrow!"

Manny stood up straight and bravely asked, "Mr. Grimes, can we please have a mango? We took care of the tree all year long. We gave the tree water…and food…and we pulled off the bugs on it. Can we have a fruit, please?"

"No!" snapped Mr. Grimes, "all the fruit belongs to the building's owner. I have my orders. Now go away!"

And he slammed the door shut.

17

Manny and Maria were sad and disappointed. "We'll never get a mango now," said Manny.

"Wait," said Maria. "I have an idea."

When Maria whispered in Manny's ear, he smiled a great big smile.

The next afternoon Manny and Maria went door to door in
their building telling the other children about their idea.

The following Saturday, from the courtyard the residents of the apartment building heard a loud chant:

"Whose tree? Our Tree! "Whose Mangoes? Our Mangoes!"

All of the children in the building were carrying signs and marching in the courtyard around the mango tree.

When Mama and Mrs. Garcia watched the children on the TV news that evening, they were proud of the little ones.

But still, they worried.

What would the owner do about all the fuss?

The next day Mr. Grimes went out to the children who were marching again in the courtyard.

"Stop the shouting!" yelled Mr. Grimes. "Well," the Super growled, "since you took care of the tree all year long, giving it water and food and picking the bugs off it, I suppose you can each have one mango."

"Yay!" All the children shouted.

"Thank you Mr. Grimes," said Manny with a wide grin. "We can eat the mangoes together."

Mama rushed to Manny and hugged him. "Papa and I are so proud of you," she said.

The next afternoon, the residents of the apartment building threw a big party. They ate Mango pies, Mango fruit sticks, Mango biscuits and Mango ice cream.

Everyone had fun at the party under the big mango tree.

Even Mr. Grimes.

Ali R., Lia, Ali & Valerie Bustamante

Monica Lunot-Kuker

BOOKS FROM HARD BALL PRESS

MANNY & THE MANGO TREE – by Ali R. & Valerie Bustamante, illustrations by Monica Lunot-Kuker

SIXTEEN TONS - An Historical Novel, by Kevin Corley

MURDER OF A POST OFFICE MANAGER – A Legal Drama by Paul Felton

WHAT DID YOU LEARN AT WORK TODAY? THE FORBIDDEN LESSONS OF LABOR EDUCATION – Nonfiction by Helena Worthen

NEW YORK HUSTLE: POOL ROOMS, SCHOOL ROOMS AND STREET CORNERS – A Memoir by Stan Maron

LOVE DIES - A Thriller by Timothy Sheard

IN HIDING – A Thriller by Timothy Sheard

WITH OUR LOVING HANDS: 1199 NURSING HOME WORKERS TELL THEIR STORY. edited by Timothy Sheard

WE ARE ONE: SELF PORTRAITS OF AMERICAN UNION MEMBERS , edited by Elizabeth Gottlieb (April 2015 release)

PASSION'S PRIDE: RETURN TO THE DAWNING – A novel by Cathie Wright-Lewis (March 2015 release)

The Lenny Moss Mysteries, by Timothy Sheard

THIS WON'T HURT A BIT
SOME CUTS NEVER HEAL
A RACE AGAINST DEATH
SLIM TO NONE
NO PLACE TO BE SICK
A BITTER PILL

Made in the USA
Charleston, SC
07 December 2014